WOOLeYCAT'S® MUSICAL THEATER

Written by Dennis Hysom & Christine Walker
Songs performed by Dennis • Paintings by Christine

 Tortuga Press • Santa Rosa, California

For Olympia

Text © 1992, 2003 Dennis Hysom and
    Christine Walker
Illustrations © 2003 Christine Walker
Music and lyrics, exclusive of
    traditional lyrics © 1992, 2003
    Dennis Hysom and Christine Walker
Inquiries should be addressed to: Tortuga Press,
PMB 181, 2777 Yulupa Avenue, Santa Rosa, California 95405, U.S.A.
Phone: 707.544.4720

The illustrations were rendered in watercolor and gouache.
The songs on the audio portion were performed by Dennis Hysom.
Book design by Christine Walker
Book production by Lynn Bell, Monroe Street Studios
Print management by The Kids at Our House

Manufactured in China

Library of Congress Cataloging-in-Publication Data

Hysom, Dennis Joe, 1949–
    Wooleycat's musical theater /written by Dennis Hysom &
Christine Walker; songs performed by Dennis ; paintings by Christine.
        p. cm.—(Wooleycat's favorite nursery rhymes)
    Summary: Expands and updates ten Mother Goose rhymes so that familiar
characters solve their own problems, find creative solutions, and discover new ways
to get along with each other.
    LCCN: 2002115684
    ISBN 1-889910-25-2—ISBN 1-889910-26-0 (pbk.)
    [1. Mother Goose—Parodies, imitations, etc.] I. Walker, Christine. II. Title.
III. Series.

PZ8.3.W985 Wo 2003
[E]—dc21
                              2002032060

WOOLEYCAT'S MUSICAL THEATER

Welcome to my tree house stage,
where everyone plays a part.
We take rhymes and make them new.
So grab a hat. Let's start!

THE
WISHING TREE

Pull Yourself Together, Humpty!

Humpty Dumpty sat on a wall.
Humpty Dumpty had a great fall.
All the king's horses and all the king's men
couldn't put Humpty Dumpty together again.

They took him to the doctor,
they took him to the baker,
they took him to the architect
and also to the tailor.

The doctor tried to sew him up—
ten stitches in a row.
The baker tried to patch him up
with egg yolks and sweet dough.

Pull...yourself together, Humpty!
(When you tumble, trip and fall.)
Pull...yourself together, Humpty!
(When you're feeling beat.)
Turn your sunny side up
and scramble to your feet!

They took him to the architect,
who measured Humpty ear to ear.
"I could build him a new shell,
but it would take at least three years!"

They took him to the tailor,
whose voice was cool and calm.
"I know a way to help him.
Make a phone call to his mom!"
Chorus

EMERGENCY

They called for Mrs. Dumpty,
who came in such a hurry.
"My, oh my! Poor Humpty!
I've been beside myself with worry!"

She knelt beside her little boy,
kissed him on the brow:

Something stirred inside his yolk
and healed him from within.
No one moved, no one spoke—
king's horse nor king's men.

Mama's here.
I love you, dear!
Are you feeling better now?

Humpty scrambled up and sang
directly from his heart:

Love and care
can pull you back
when you fall apart!

Pull...yourself together, Humpty!
(When you tumble, trip and fall.)
Pull...yourself together, Humpty!
(When you're feeling beat.)
Turn your sunny side up
and scramble to your feet!

Miss Muffet's *Mmmm* Berry Pie

Little Miss Muffet sat on a tuffet,
eating her curds and whey.
Along came a spider, who sat down beside her
and frightened Miss Muffet away.

The spider was an itty-bitty baker
with a twinkle in his itty-bitty eye.
He only came down to borrow some sugar
to sweeten his berry pie.

Mmmm berry pie! Mmmm berry pie!
Put it in the oven and it comes out hot!
Can't get enough of that berry pie—
Thanks a lot!

"Hey, hey, little Miss Muffet,
I'm just a spider, that's all.
You've got feet to walk around,
but I can only crawl.

"You know I never tried to hurt you,
so don't you run away and cry,
'cause if I can't borrow some sugar from you,
there'll be no berry pie!" **Chorus**

So little Miss Muffet wiped the tears from her eyes.
"Berry pie, did you say?
Well, that's my favorite, little one.
Let's bake it together today!"

So they became the best of friends,
and now you know the reason why.
It wasn't because they changed who they were,
but because they both loved berry pie.

Mmmm berry pie! Mmmm berry pie!
Put it in the oven and it comes out hot!
Can't get enough of that berry pie—
Thanks a lot!

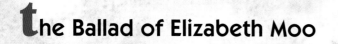the Ballad of Elizabeth Moo

Hey diddle, diddle!
The cat and the fiddle,
the cow jumped up over the moon.
The little dog laughed
just to see such a sport,
and the dish ran away with the spoon.

Now, hey diddle, diddle!
There's more to the riddle:
the dish with the spoon got caught;
the cow's real name was Elizabeth Moo,
and she became an astronaut.

America sent her off into space
to talk with the man in the moon.
She said, "Tell me your view
of the earth far below,"
then he sang her this wonderful tune:

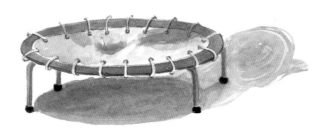

One world,
one place,
one home for
the human race.
Now you see it.
Now you don't.
Be careful!
It's something
you can't
replace!

Lizzie flew close
to the man in the moon,
then he whispered into her ear,
"It's only a fragile spinning ball
when you look at Earth from up here!"

"This is mission control, Liz.
We read you loud and clear.
What the man in the moon says is very true.
Please give him our thanks and come on home.
We have a lot of work to do."

Hey diddle, diddle!
The cat played the fiddle
as Lizzie flew home from the moon.
The little dog marched with the big brass band.
They all sang this wonderful tune:

One world,
one place,
one home for
the human race.
Now you see it.
Now you don't.
Be careful!
It's something
you can't
replace!

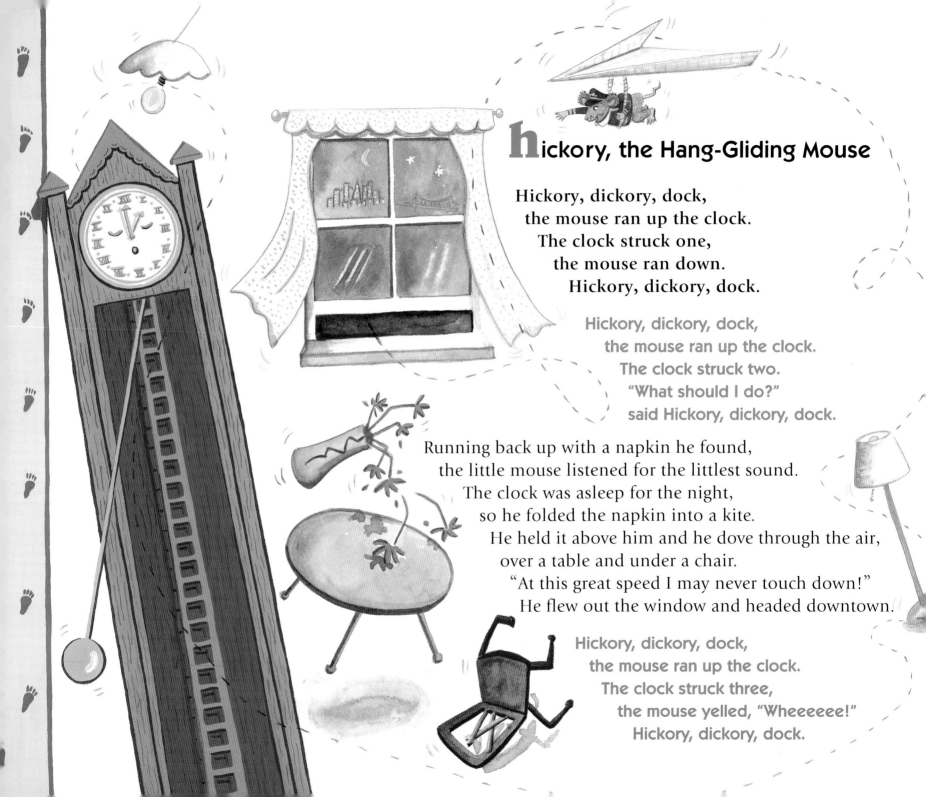

hickory, the Hang-Gliding Mouse

Hickory, dickory, dock,
the mouse ran up the clock.
The clock struck one,
the mouse ran down.
Hickory, dickory, dock.

Hickory, dickory, dock,
the mouse ran up the clock.
The clock struck two.
"What should I do?"
said Hickory, dickory, dock.

Running back up with a napkin he found,
the little mouse listened for the littlest sound.
The clock was asleep for the night,
so he folded the napkin into a kite.
He held it above him and he dove through the air,
over a table and under a chair.
"At this great speed I may never touch down!"
He flew out the window and headed downtown.

Hickory, dickory, dock,
the mouse ran up the clock.
The clock struck three,
the mouse yelled, "Wheeeeee!"
Hickory, dickory, dock.

He flew over rooftops and people asleep.
No one could hear his little voice peep,
"Help! I can't get this thing down!"
Suddenly a kind breeze turned him around.
It carried him back through the cold, cold night.
His cozy, warm house was a wonderful sight.
Tired and cold from his ears to his toes,
he shivered as he yelled,
"Oh! The window's closed!"

Hickory, dickory, dock,
the mouse ran up the clock.
The clock struck four,
here's a little more,
Hickory, dickory, dock.

He crawled back home on his four shaky feet;
little gray mouse was white as a sheet.
The clock in the house laughed all through the night
at the thought of a mouse on a hang-gliding kite.

Hickory, dickory, dock,

he still runs up the clock,

but that's all he'll do

when the clock strikes two,

Hickory, dickory, dock.

the Adventures of Mary and Her Lamb

Mary had a little lamb,
its fleece was white as snow.
And everywhere that Mary went
the lamb was sure to go.

They went dancing in Paris
(the lamb did the Charleston).

They went sailing through the South Seas
(Mary rode a surfboard).

They played baseball with their old friends
(the lamb hit a home run).

They baked pizza and lasagne
(Mary knew the recipes).

And the lamb sang:

Mary's a friend of mine,
we play together all the time.
Great friends are hard to find.
Mary's a friend of mine!

He followed her to class each day,
which was against the rules.
He learned to read and write in this way.
He liked to go to school.
Chorus

three Blind Mice on Vacation in Africa

Three blind mice on vacation in Africa
bumped into a great big elephant.
"What can this be?"
"Let's inspect it and see!"
said the three blind mice.

The first blind mouse touched the elephant's knee.
"This must be the trunk of a very old tree!"
"Let's climb to the top to see what we can see!"
said the three blind mice.

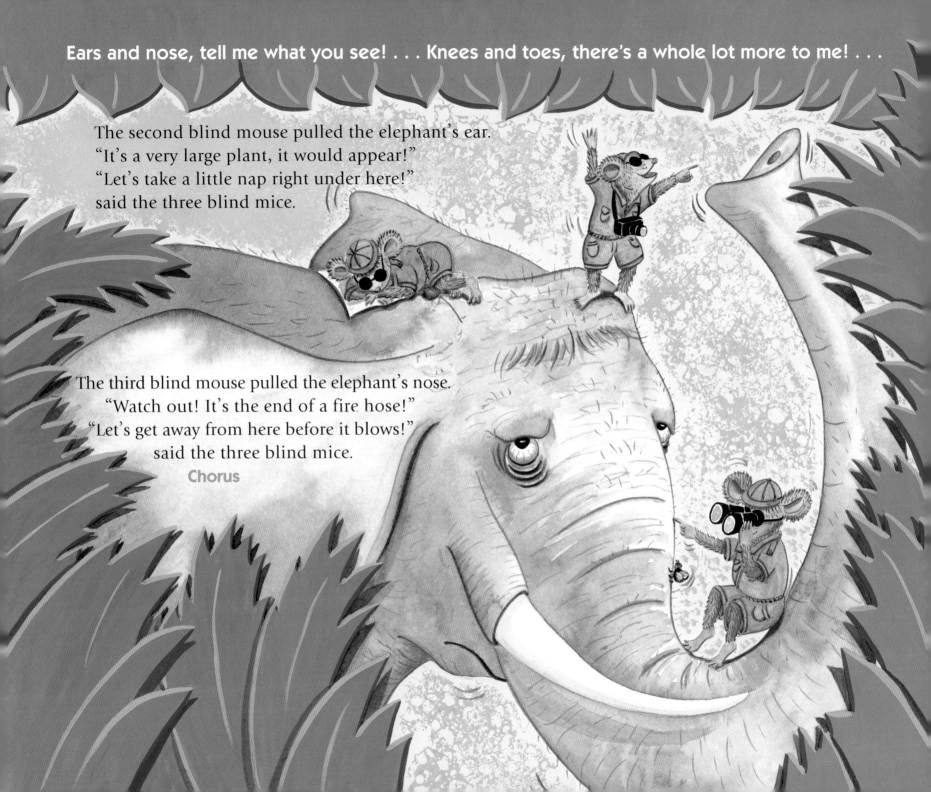

Ears and nose, tell me what you see! . . . Knees and toes, there's a whole lot more to me! . . .

The second blind mouse pulled the elephant's ear.
"It's a very large plant, it would appear!"
"Let's take a little nap right under here!"
said the three blind mice.

The third blind mouse pulled the elephant's nose.
"Watch out! It's the end of a fire hose!"
"Let's get away from here before it blows!"
said the three blind mice.
Chorus

1adybug, the Famous Firefighter

**Ladybug, Ladybug, fly away home.
Your house is on fire!**

She puts on her big black boots
and her firefighter's hat—
down the pole and out the door
in thirty seconds flat!

She grabs her shiny overcoat,
turns on the flashing light.
Out rolls the great red engine.
She'll put out a fire tonight!

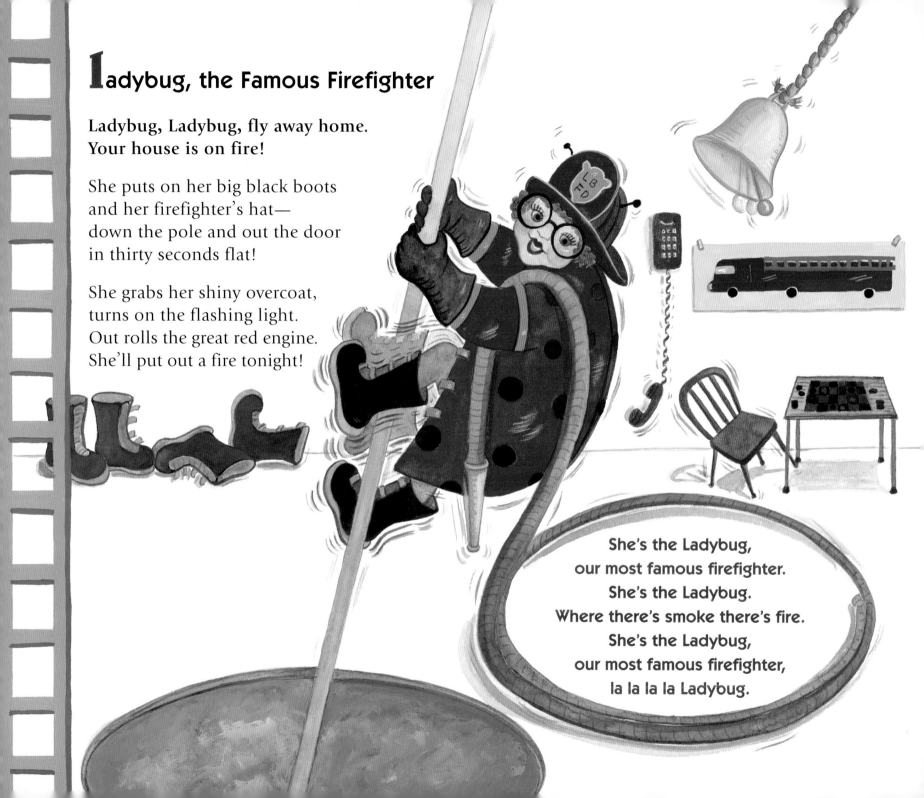

She's the Ladybug,
our most famous firefighter.
She's the Ladybug.
Where there's smoke there's fire.
She's the Ladybug,
our most famous firefighter,
la la la la Ladybug.

Fire bells echo through the night.
They ring with urgency.
The neighbors wake up and run to help.
It's an emergency!

She sets up the sturdy ladder,
hooks up the thirsty hose.
She turns on the fire hydrant.
Whoosh! The water! Out it goes!

She's the Ladybug,
our most famous firefighter.
She's the Ladybug.
Where there's smoke there's fire.
She's the Ladybug,
our most famous firefighter,
la la la la Ladybug.

"Put out the fire, Ladybug!"
her neighbors jump and shout.
Ladybug aims that hose just right.
Whoosh! "Hooray! The fire's out!"
Chorus

I Saw a Ship a-Sailin'

I saw a ship a-sailin', a-sailin' on the sea,
and, oh, it was all laden with pretty things for thee.
There were comfits in the cabin and apples in the hold.
The sails were made of silk and the masts were made of gold.

The four and twenty sailors stood waiting down below.
They were four and twenty white mice, each ready set to row.
The captain was a duck with a packet on his back,
and when the ship began to move, the captain said,

Quack! Quack!

I took that ship a-sailin', a-sailin' out to sea,
and, oh, it was a pleasure with treasures all for thee.
The ship she sailed so gently on waves deep green and blue.
The sailors sang a chantey as we sailed home to you.

"We're sailing the seas in a wooden boat
with twenty-four sailors to row.
We'll catch a fine wind and away we'll float,
and we'll be home tomorrow.

"Hey! Ho! Sing it low,
we've got miles and miles to go.
Hey! Hi! Sing it fine,
we'll be home by suppertime!"

jack and Jill's Better Scheme

Jack and Jill went up the hill
to fetch a pail of water.
Jack fell down and broke his crown,
and Jill came tumbling after.

Up the hill, down the hill,
they tried to climb all day;
but Jack and Jill kept tumbling down.
There's got to be a better way!

SLIPPERY SLOPE

Inside out, upside down,
pick up your problem and turn it around.
Down side up, inside out,
play with it, stay with it, work it all out!

"Jill," said Jack, "this hill's too steep.
What we need is a better scheme."
"You're right," said Jill. "Forget the hill.
Let's go find a little stream." **Chorus**

They found a stream so sparkling clean,
and they drank their fill.
There are many ways to get what you need,
so take a tip from Jack and Jill.

Willie Winkie's Bedtime Surprise

Wee Willie Winkie runs through the town,
upstairs and downstairs in his nightgown;
rapping at the windows,
crying at the locks,
"Are you children fast asleep?
For now it's eight o'clock!"

"Yes, Willie. We're asleep...."

He knows they're hiding under pillows.
They're all wound up in sheets—
cold noses, warm toes and tiny little feet.
They're cuddled up and snuggled down,
hugging furry things.
The kids are very quiet now—
too quiet, Willie thinks!

So he looks in every window:
there are shadows on the floor.
He looks around, then carefully
he opens up the door.
He races up the stairway,
stumbles down the hall.
    "Is everybody sleeping?"
        the children hear him call.

"Hey, Wee Willie Winkie,
yes, we're sound asleep!
Close the door,
we're busy counting sheep.
Hey, Wee Willie Winkie,
we're resting very well.
Please quiet down, we're sleeping,
can't you tell?"

He hears noises in the darkness,
there's something in the air.
A shadow in the corner reminds him of a bear.
He thinks he sees a giant, or could it be an elf?
Or a monkey or a kangaroo jumping off the shelf?

Now the room is full of dragons, crocodiles and owls,
roars and hoots and screeches and tiny little growls.
Willie turns the light on, and no one makes a peep.
"Are you children tricking me, or are you fast asleep?"

"Hey, Wee Willie Winkie,
yes, we're sound asleep!
Close the door,
we're busy counting sheep.
Hey, Wee Willie Winkie,
we're resting very well.
Please quiet down, we're sleeping,
can't you tell?"

Wee Willie Winkie runs through the town,
upstairs and downstairs in his nightgown;
rapping at the windows, turning out the lights.
"Are you children fast asleep? It's almost midnight!"

"Yes, Willie. We're asleep!"

THE END

Ticket
to
Rhyme

Ticket
to
Rhyme

Ticket
to
Rhyme

Ticket
to
Rhyme

Ticket
to
Rhyme

Ticket
to
Rhyme

Ticket
to
Rhyme

Ticket
to
Rhyme

Ticket
to
Rhyme

Ticket
to
Rhyme

Ticket
to
Rhyme

Ticket
to
Rhyme

Ticket
to
Rhyme

Ticket
to
Rhyme